BLACKTOP

JANAE

For ELK—here is your love letter—LA

GROSSET & DUNLAP
Penguin Young Readers Group
An Imprint of Penguin Random House LLC

Text copyright © 2016 by Penguin Random House LLC. Cover illustration copyright
© 2016 by Raul Allen. All rights reserved. Published by Grosset & Dunlap,
an imprint of Penguin Random House LLC, 345 Hudson Street, New York, New
York 10014. GROSSET & DUNLAP is a trademark of Penguin Random House LLC.
Printed in the USA.

Library of Congress Cataloging-in-Publication Data is available.

ISBN 9781101995648 (paperback)   10 9 8 7 6 5 4 3 2 1
ISBN 9780399542763 (library binding)   10 9 8 7 6 5 4 3 2 1

BLACKTOP

JANAE

BY LJ ALONGE

Grosset & Dunlap
An Imprint of Penguin Random House

Basketball chooses you. It's just one of life's mysteries—like the existence of yawning or gravity—a thing no middle-school science teacher has been able to explain for ten thousand years. But everybody who hoops remembers the exact moment they were chosen. It gets tattooed in capital letters somewhere deep in the animal part of your memory, the same part of your brain that remembers your first crush. You show up to the park on a summer morning planning to put up a few jumpers, just for fun. Maybe practice a little crossover or reverse layup you saw on TV the night before. You make a bunch of shots, you miss a bunch—everything's good. Except: It's early, and you've got time, so why not put up a few more jumpers? And you do that. And you feel good enough to put up a few more, and a few more after that. And then, without even realizing it, you've left the planet. You're somewhere else.

In this new world, it doesn't matter that your arms and legs are deadweight, or that the back of your neck's been on fire for hours, or that your mouth is Sahara-dry, or that your stomach's rattling around in your abdomen like a pebble in a shoe. Doesn't matter that your ball's flat, the court's cracked, the rim's crooked. Doesn't matter that you were supposed to be home three hours ago. Doesn't matter how many you've made, how many you've missed. You've left Earth, and on your new planet, living means putting the ball through the hoop. A few more times. And a few more times after that.

When you do finally get home, you wash up, you eat, you do chores, you lie down. It should feel normal, but it doesn't. Your granny asks what's wrong, but what can you say? You've got a roof and a bed and a full stomach—you should be happy. All you know is that something's off. Home doesn't feel like home; it just feels like a place to rest, somewhere to wait around, a bus stop. Usually you can fall right to sleep, but on this night, you can't. Since there's nothing like a sleepless night for some philosophizing, it hits you that "home" is just where you feel most comfortable, the place that makes you feel the most like yourself. The place that makes you feel the most free. That place, you suddenly realize, is the blacktop. Out there on the blacktop, with the sun beating down on you, and your shot clanking off the rim, and your feet throbbing, you felt free for the first time in your life. Really truly free.

That's how you know you've been chosen. And when you're chosen, there's no turning back. From then on, forever, the game has you.

Granny likes the Strange Goods

Superstore to open at sunrise. Of course that doesn't mean she's the one doing the opening. Earlier, as the sky went from black to foamy gray, she turned up the TV to ear-splitting volume and shuffled loudly into the bathroom. I was already awake, listening to her run the bathwater, hoping she wouldn't call out to me.

"Get up, Janae!" she yelled, her voice made deep and monstrous by the steam. "You ain't here on vacation."

She hates it when I sleep late, and so I lay there, quiet and defiant. A few minutes later I could feel the air mattress shake as she marched down the hall. When she threw open my door, I only saw her outline. Her squat body filled the doorway like an eclipse, blocking out the light from the hall.

I pretended to be asleep, watching her with my eyes barely open.

"You swear you're the slickest kid in this whole world," she said, flicking on the lights.

Now I'm sitting behind the register downstairs, trapped in that annoying spot between wakefulness and sleep. Right about now I'd kill for the thin, scratchy sheets on the guest bed, the same sheets my mom used when she was a kid. I put my head on the counter, and the glass holding our Weird Souvenirs collection cools my cheek. The lights are dim (we tell people it's for the protection of our most delicate items), and suddenly I feel my eyelids getting heavy. I won't fight it. No one's coming in any time soon. Between lazy blinks I can make out the idling garbage trucks and taxis on the street, big clouds of exhaust chugging out of their tailpipes. It'll be a few hours before the other stores roll up their steel gates and begin selling their conventional wares, their buttoned-up customers passing by our windows with curious glances. Our customers, like our hours, are strange.

The bells on our front door wake me up. I don't know how long I've been out. A cold burst of air knifes in, and behind it is Ms. Evans. She unwraps the thick scarf covering her nose and mouth. She's scowling, the deep wrinkles in her face crumpled into an angry mask.

"This doesn't work," she moans.

She slams down a multicolored wooden ring, and it spins on the glass counter like a top. Purple swirls of ancient-looking text run down both sides. On top is a cracked green jewel. Small splinters of wood splay out from the band. It's from our igneous rock line.

"Sure it does," I say, yawning for effect.

She folds her arms. "Then how come I don't feel any better?"

"Our policy, Ms. Evans." I point to the eye-level sign written in all caps behind me: NO REFUNDS.

Ms. Evans is our most loyal customer. She's here every day, rubbing our lucky rabbits' feet on the nape of her neck, weighing the steel pieces of our antique Ouija boards, flipping through our dusty treasure maps. It didn't take much work to sell her the scarf she's currently wearing.

We tell people it's made from Himalayan cotton, grown in the thinnest air humans can breathe and spun by the expert hands of lady Sherpas. I'd rubbed it on her cheek and told her the scarves improved circulation, feeling guilty as I watched her eyes light up with wonder. She bought five of them, and I helped her wrap the other four for her grandkids. Lying to her makes me feel crappy, and that, I'm now realizing, makes me angry.

I sigh. "Try putting it on a different finger."

She holds out her brown, liver-spotted hands and wiggles her fingers. "Which one?"

"Any. Doesn't matter."

"Well, if this one isn't working . . ." She pauses. Her fingers flutter above the glass.

Below the glass sit orderly rows of gold-colored rings and bracelets; the little signs attached to them say they dramatically improve mood, joint health, and sexual stamina. Granny expects these to sell fast. "Maybe I should just get another one?"

I want to grab her by the shoulders and shake her. *Ms. Evans, who told you to believe in this crap?* I wonder. *You won Science Teacher of the Year three times. You have a daughter who's a doctor and a son who's a detective. You once showed me how the inside of a watch works.*

She's bent over, staring through the glass, her lips parted as she reads the signs. I can see her pulse through the thin, waxy skin on her neck. Her wig is slightly crooked under her hat.

"Well," she says, "I *do* need more stamina."

"Here," I groan, grabbing the tray of rings, "let's look at a few things from our new collection."

I wait until Ms. Evans leaves to slam the register. I hate it here. I hate the wobbly, three-legged stool behind the register. I hate the stinky fly traps we keep near the bathroom, the off-key bells on the front door. Outside, with the fog rolling away, everything looks soft-edged and warm. If life were fair, I'd be out there playing twenty-one until my hands got calloused. I'd be talking shit to the boys who never put me on their team. I'd snarl at the girls who glare at me, as if I wanted their knock-kneed boyfriends.

But Granny's grooming me to be the next manager, and that means I work long hours cheating people out of their money.

The Strange Goods Superstore was opened by Granny twenty years ago. According to our sign, we're "proud purveyors of the peculiar." Walk down one aisle and you'll find volcanic stones that boost energy. In the next you'll find a pile of water diviners stacked together in a thorny mess. Our Egyptian salts, supposedly aged for hundreds of years in the tombs of pharaohs, are locally famous. When used in your bath, they're supposed to make you appear younger. And if you bring in any of Granny's numerous profiles from the local paper, you get a 10 percent discount.

Every summer my sisters and I are

shipped up here to restock the dream catchers and healing cloths, the prosperity purses and books on elementary divination. I used to love it. Granny would sit at the register humming upbeat jazz songs. Vanilla incense wafted out of the front doors. Old dreadlocked guys would sit on the sidewalk just outside, smoking weed out of handmade pipes and eating sugar-free cookies. Granny would have to drag me by my collar to bed.

But one unusually warm night last summer I went to the kitchen for some juice, and there she was, boiling down a big pot of Morton table salt.

"What?" she asked, turning up the heat. "Santa ain't real, either."

Granny says she wouldn't trust my sisters to spot the stripes on a zebra. That means I'm the sweet-faced front for the whole operation, the one she plans to leave all of this to. Now I do all the restocking, returns, opening, closing, and bookkeeping. It's joyless, guilt-inducing work. A dozen Ms. Evanses come in every day, looking for answers to failing marriages and arteries, out-of-control colons and kids.

Now that I do all the work, Granny stays in our apartment upstairs. Lately I've been starting to worry about her. She paces around the living room all night, chain-smoking and binge-watching *Unsolved Crimes*. Whenever they find the perp, she shakes her head and looks through the blinds suspiciously.

"Don't you want to go somewhere?" I asked once.

Ghostly light from the TV washed across her face. "With what money?"

"I thought you had money, Granny."

Her laugh is bitter and phlegmy. I suddenly remember the gallon of quarters and half dollars in the back of her closet— my college fund.

"Okay," I say, "let's say the store made a bunch of money."

"Unlikely!"

"Let's say I make it playing basketball. We could go anywhere you want."

"Ha!"

"What's so funny about that?"

"A boy's game?" Granny asked. "You want to make a life playing a boy's game? This right here, *this* is life."

CHAPTER 2
ANYTHING FOR HOOP

My boys come in the afternoons,
drunk on sunshine and freedom. Ever since
the game against Ghosttown—we lost,
but not as bad as everyone thought we
would—they've been on a kind of victory
tour. They spend all day at Rasputin Music
in Berkeley or the mildewy comic stores in
the Mission, telling younger kids about the
importance of perseverance and hard work.
They wander around the farmers' markets
like kings, raiding the free samples of
avocado and mango. Today Frank opens the

door, and Justin walks in holding a giant stuffed koala.

"Look at what this guy won," Frank says.

Justin holds the koala over his head.

"We're at the fair," Frank continues, "and he walks up to that milk-bottle game—the one where you have to throw the ball at them? For sure the ball's going into the parking lot, right? Oh no! Dude knocks down every bottle, gets a koala. Why the hell did you get a koala?"

Justin holds the koala like a game-show host, his smile big and dopey. Then he lowers it and hands it to me, too shy to look me in the eye. Frank looks back and forth between us, no stranger to the silent workings of romance. I watch him as he moonwalks down the International aisle, making vigorous pumping motions with his hips.

"I got this for you," Justin says, once Frank's out of earshot.

"Um, thanks."

"You like koalas, right?"

"Not really." I pick up the koala by the ear and put it under the register. I can't help being awful to him. At fifteen, I'm all too familiar with the sky-high price of love. My sisters are twins, four years older than me, and the kind of girls who giggle when someone tells them they have beautiful cheekbones. It's like the part of me that likes Justin and the part of me that doesn't trust boys are at war.

"I mean," Justin says, "we could go back to the fair and you could show me what you want and I bet they'd let me exchange it or I could win another one or—"

"Can't," I say, leaning on the register. "Gotta stay here, sell stuff."

"Oh. Right. Duh." His shoulders droop, and he suddenly looks much smaller, totally harmless. "Never mind, then."

We look around the store, searching for something to talk about. Sometimes he asks me about our dream catchers and tie-dyed sweaters, if there's anything we have for righting a really, really bad wrong. Then I get so close to telling him it's all a sham, anyway, I have to actually bite my tongue. I'm hoping he brings up a game happening tonight. Most nights, I wait for Granny to fall asleep before I grab my sneakers and take the bus to wherever the boys are.

There's always a good run somewhere: the Lake on Saturdays, San Leandro on Wednesdays, Alameda on Fridays.

"Is there a game tonight?" I hear myself say.

Justin's face brightens. "We're actually going up to Berkeley today."

We usually play in Fruitvale on Thursdays. "What's in Berkeley?"

"Somebody has an open gym. I was thinking you might wanna play inside for a change."

Justin looks at me and looks at me and looks at me. This time I'm the one who can't look back. It's not the greedy look I get from the some of the clowns who come in off the street, the ones with the same greasy line about showing me their personal "magic."

Justin's look is different, the kind of lost, watery-eyed look my sisters get when they're up to their necks in blankets, on the phone with a boy they really like.

"What time?" I ask, trying to hold back my giddiness.

I decide that it's closing time. Foot traffic has dwindled to zilch. Streetlights flicker on, illuminating fingerlike waves of fog rolling past the front door. I think of the smoky bars my sister are probably in, standing in wobbly heels, laughing hysterically as they twirl their braids around their fingers. I take the money out of the register and order it the way Granny likes, small bills on top. Eighty-seven dollars, all ones, fives, and tens. She'll count it again when I give it to her, and if she's in a good mood, she'll peel off a few bills for me. I glance at the door leading to Granny's apartment. What if she's mad about how much I made? I can't risk missing tonight. Well, I consider, let's think: Today definitely wasn't a bad day. Some people might even call it a *good* day. A *super* good day if I count the lady with the thyroid problem who didn't have cash and said she'd come back tomorrow to buy up the store. Can't forget about her. So: If I asked, Granny would probably give me at *least* twenty bucks for all my hard work. Right. I generously peel off a ten and slip it into my pocket.

"You're too much like me," Granny once told me. She'd caught me stealing one of her hand-rolled cigarettes. I was shaking so bad, all the tobacco had fallen onto the floor.

"Here," she said. She refilled the cigarette and lit the open end. "Here's your glory." She made me smoke it until I threw up. I'd laid in bed in a ball, praying she'd be struck by lightning.

She moved a bucket next to the bed and spoke in a whisper. "Yeah, I was just like you"—she was sitting at the end of the bed, rubbing my feet—"always running to trouble. We've got it in us, our family. The Jenkins women. Can't help it."

Granny's had more lives than most. Before she owned the store, she was a lounge singer. She can still hit the high notes, in case anyone asks. She's lived in seven states, in salt-sprayed villas on Miami Beach and trailer parks a stone's throw from

Tijuana. She ditched three husbands, just up and left when she got bored or they got crazy. The best place to hide from yourself, she once told me, is in the middle of a club, right in front of everybody.

When I get upstairs she's in her usual spot on the La-Z-Boy, her hand a vise grip around the remote. Every few moments she twitches like she's dreaming of something bad, her braless breasts crawling around under her nightgown like groundhogs. Her favorite crime show is on TV. This episode is about a shady banker who steals a gajillion dollars and then outruns the Coast Guard to Cuba in his supercharged yacht. Streams of bills fly off the deck and into the ocean, and he turns back to try to use a net to scoop it all up.

I try to slip the stack of money under Granny's ashtray, but it lands with a thud and startles her awake. She drops the remote and looks around, wild-eyed, breathing fast. I stay crouched near her feet, too afraid to move. I hold my breath until I can feel the air about to burst out of my throat. Then she collapses back into her chair, and I wait until she starts snoring again before I crawl out the front door on my hands and knees.

CHAPTER 3
HOOP DREAMS

No two basketball courts are alike. Each has its own flavor, its own little quirks you have to know if you want to play like yourself. Sometimes it's a rim that makes the ball bounce funny, or there's a bubble under the wood, or the lighting's too bright or too dim, or it's so humid you can't grip the ball the way you want. As far as I can see, this gym is perfect: The hardwood's springy, the air-conditioning's working, the rims look forgiving. My guys aren't here yet. I walk past a couple full-court games—

they're all standing around, arguing about fouls—to an empty half-court in the back of the gym.

Starting in the corner, I shoot until I make it, and then I take a small step right and shoot, and then another step, until I've gone all the way around the three-point line. They say you should visualize the ball going through, and that's what I do. Then I start over, taking small steps in the direction I came from. Watching the ball go through the hoop never gets old. I'm happy.

When I'm done warming up, I walk over to a shrimpy kid at one of the far courts. He has to crane his neck to look me in the eye. I pull out a sweaty five-dollar bill.

"You beat me," I say, "and it's yours."

He looks around in shock, like he's

wondering if anyone is seeing this. "You might as well hand it over now," he says.

The nerve of this kid. "You got five?"

He pulls out some ones and change.

"Matter of fact," I say, "I'll give you five bucks if you score."

The game doesn't last long enough for me to break a sweat. By the time I finish him off with a foul-line jumper, his face is ashen, like he's seen a ghost. He doesn't even look at the rim to see if the ball goes in. Instead, he stomps off the court, throwing down his money so that I have to walk around to pick it up. Ten minutes later he comes back with his friend, some kid wearing a headband and mouth guard, and I beat him, too. Then that kid's friend steps up to me. I'm up fifty bucks when I hear someone bouncing a ball behind me.

"So you think you can shoot," a voice says.

I don't turn around. "A little busy here."

"How about a little competition? Winner gets something way more than five bucks."

Now I turn around.

"A little competition," he repeats. "Winner gets a prize."

You must be kidding, I think. He's a little guy in a bright yellow tracksuit; his pants stop just above his ankles. Bald as a basketball. He makes me think of elderly substitute teachers, the ones who sit in front of the class doing a crossword puzzle, too frightened to speak. He dribbles the ball once, and it seems to surprise him when it snaps back into his hand.

"What's the prize?" I ask, pretending to be uninterested.

"You'll see when you win." He shoots, a steep, looping arc on the way to the basket, and the ball clanks off the side of the backboard, toward me. I hand him the ball. He smells like laundry detergent, like easy money.

"Let's do it," I say.

It's a race, he explains. First to ten makes. All net or it doesn't count. Get your own rebound. His voice has cooled off, gotten hard. He sounds, for the first time, like he knows what he's talking about, like maybe he's done this before. We take up positions on opposite sides of the court. I lock in, I visualize. The sounds on the other side of the gym—someone fouled someone else too hard—begin to fade. My fingers slot into the ball's familiar grooves. I look at the front of the rim like all the great shooters say you're supposed to. I'm not nervous. I've hit thousands of jumpers, in the rain, in swirling winds coming off the bay, on outdoor courts with no lights. My first shot goes up, and the net makes that sharp splashing sound.

The bald guy's ball does the same. And from the way he's made eight shots in a row without breaking a sweat, it's pretty clear I've been suckered. All that bumbling earlier was Oscar-worthy. Now he holds his ball so I can catch up a little, and I start rushing my shots, missing more, wincing when the ball clangs off the rim. I feel my hands getting sweaty, slick. Finally, he puts me out of my misery: He sends up his tenth shot and keeps his arm outstretched as it goes through.

"No hard feelings," he says. He isn't even sweating. He reaches up to pat me on the shoulder. I step back and tell him that was bullshit.

"You want to play again?" he asks.

"Best two out of three," I say.

He beats me again.

"*Now* do you want to know what the winner gets?" he says, smiling.

I'm not stupid. I'm not going to follow him down some dark alley. And besides, I'm tall enough to see the baldest spot on the top of his head. He couldn't drag me off anywhere if he wanted to. But he's spinning the ball on his finger, and I'm so curious I can't help myself. I ask him what he gets.

"You'll be coming to the Bay Area Ballers tryouts," he says.

I take a step back. "The what?" I ask, although I know exactly what that is.

"They start this Saturday at seven. The Bay Area Ballers are the premier—"

I hold up my hand. The truth is I don't need an explanation. The Bay Area Ballers only send their players to colleges that matter: UConn, Tennessee, UCLA, Baylor, Notre Dame. Playing with them is almost a guarantee that you'll get a scholarship. I've watched their games on ESPN.

"So you'll be there?" he asks.

"Are you, like, the coach or something?"

"I help out."

"And you're inviting me?"

"Yup."

"Even though I lost?"

"Yup."

"Why?"

He shrugs. "Just something about you."

That night I play out of my mind. The rim is Hula-Hoop big. Every time I make a shot I picture myself in the black Ballers uniform, an announcer with a big silky voice shouting my name.

Now that we've all been playing for a while we work like a unit, with every one of us knowing our place. I get giddy just stepping onto the court with Justin, Frank, Adrian, and Mike. Sometimes you hear an announcer talk about how a team is like an organism, and I thought it was the corniest thing until Ms. Dobb's biology class last semester. We learned about cells, how each part of a cell has to function for the whole thing to work. The nucleus makes the ribosomes, the ribosomes make the proteins, the endoplasmic reticulum carries the proteins. Under the microscope, a cell dances happily, shimmying inside its cell wall. We hum along, beating teams that are bigger and older and stronger, because we know one another.

We stay on the court for four hours, not losing once.

"Something's gotten into you," Mike says, sneaking up behind me at the water fountain.

I jump. "Just felt it today."

He puts his finger to his lips and narrows his eyes. "No, something happened. You have a look in your eyes."

What can I say? They'd never speak to me if they knew I was leaving the team now, right when we're getting good. I splash some water in my mouth and look at him with my best poker face. "What look?"

"The same look I had when I got my show. The way you look when you think you've found the answer to all your problems."

CHAPTER 4

GOING, GOING, GONE

"No more basketball," Granny says. It's morning. I got up early, still buzzing from last night. She's not happy with what I made yesterday. "We miss out on customers when you close the shop early."

"But, Granny—"

She holds up her hand. "Take it up with God. I need you here." I know there's no point in arguing. Granny's lived too hard a life—Jim Crow, the LA riots, the Loma Prieta earthquake—to take anybody's complaints seriously. If you're not on your deathbed, she's not trying to hear it. I slam the door on the way out.

The morning goes by slowly. In the afternoon I sit on the sidewalk outside, watching the squirrels run up the telephone poles and over the power lines. The fog stays clamped down like a lid. I could run away, I think. Like in those stories about a sad kid with a third arm who runs away to join the circus. But where would I go? What would I do? I've got no skills except working a register, making honor roll, and playing basketball. I doubt I'd make it past the city limits without accidentally eating some poisonous berries. I shudder.

Later on Ms. Evans walks in with her son, the cop. Ms. Evans is thin-limbed and spry, but he holds the crook of her arm as they walk around the store, anyway. It's his first time here, and the way he pinches our fabrics and looks over his shoulder like something's about to jump out at him—it makes me nervous.

"Nothing for you?" I ask sweetly when they come to the front of the store. Ms. Evans wants to buy a special hand-pressed rosehip oil that is really just canola Granny added some red food coloring to.

"So how can you prove that everything here does what you say it does?" He picks up one of our healing bracelets and then throws it down into the pile and wipes his hand on his shirt.

"All of it has the stamp of approval from my grandmother." That's what I've been told to say. People still love Granny. The other day they did a write-up of her in the paper, celebrating her twenty years of business. There's talk of a potential mural in an alley down the street.

"Yeah, but I want to know if you have any evidence"—he takes the bottle of oil out of his mother's hand and holds it under a lamp—"that using this actually adds five to ten years to your life."

"Hush," Ms. Evans says. "This place has done a lot for me."

Her son folds his arms, his large biceps tensing. After they walk out, he throws his hands up and points back at me, yelling things I'm too far away to hear.

Granny's up when I get upstairs, for a change. She may be a hag who wants to kill my dreams, but I still love her. I tell her about Ms. Evans and her son.

"Ha," Granny says, rolling a cigarette.

"You're not worried?"

"Dealt with a whole lot worse than a meathead mama's boy."

"So what do I do if he comes back?"

"What kind of stupid question is that? Try to sell him something!"

He comes back the next day, wearing sunglasses, as if I wouldn't recognize him. The sight of him gives me a bad-seafood feeling somewhere deep in my gut. I pretend to restock some candles as I follow him from aisle to aisle.

"You're a cop, right?" I ask.

"Have we met before?" he asks.

"You were in here yesterday with Ms. Evans."

He takes off his sunglasses and squints at me. His eyes are bloodshot. "Yes."

"So maybe you're looking for, like, a mug or something? We've got some mugs."

He smiles a big, unsettling smile. "Really? And what special powers do those have?"

I give him one of the mugs. The clay has big cracks, fault lines running up and down that make it look a lot older than it really is. "The volcanic clay in these helps with oral and digestive health."

"Where's the owner of this place?"

"Why?"

"I'd like to ask her some questions directly."

Sometimes you don't know what to do and you end up doing the dumbest thing possible. I go upstairs and ask Granny if she can answer some questions.

"Sorry," I say when I get back downstairs. My ear burns from Granny pinching it, and I try to hide the fact that I really want to rub it. "She's not here."

"Are you sure?" he asks.

I nod eagerly. "Yup, I checked."

"Well, I hope you find her." The mug slips out of his hands and shatters into a million pieces on the linoleum.

"Maybe I can answer some questions! What do you want to know?" I yell, stepping over the clay and following him outside. "Where are you going? Somebody has to pay for that mug!"

Later this morning our neighbor Mr. Graham has a heart attack during Zumba class. Two cop cars jump the curb right outside our store with sirens blaring. An ambulance speeds up behind them, and two burly guys in all white rush into the gym across the street. All of us on the block watch as they wheel Mr. Graham out on a stretcher. It's a minor attack; he gives a thumbs-up and takes off his oxygen mask to remind us of the importance of daily exercise. I think of Granny and what would happen if she had a heart attack, if she'd demand that they let her take her smokes. When I get upstairs, the door's wide open. The TV is off. Granny is not in her La-Z-Boy. A cigarette smolders in the ashtray, and under the ashtray is a note:

Could feel the heat from up here
Don't be mad will be back soon (I
bet you didn't know this old lady
could still cut and run if she had to!)
Make sure to keep the store open like
we talked about I don't want to hear
about my store being closed check the
fridge for rice if your hungry when you
see your sisters tell them I ain't too old
to give them a spanking because from
what I'm hearing that's what they
asking for

Gone is the sweet-smelling lavender oil she uses for her morning baths. Gone is my milk-jug college fund. Gone are the stacked photocopies of newspaper profiles Granny liked to pass out to people who walked past her store. Every picture makes her look like the sweetest old lady.

The best place to hide is right in front of everybody. I leave the store open all day, because I know it's what Granny would want. Tonight I decide to check out Granny's old haunts. I don't want to look for her, but I know she hates the idea of me *not* looking for her whenever she up and leaves. She couldn't have gone far this time, not with that bad leg. Outside, the moon hangs low and yellow like a dingy lightbulb. Cold nips at my calves. I'm in one of my sisters' dresses, so thin it surprises me every time the winds blows it against the backs of my legs. If the twins see me, they'll try to snatch the dress off my back—I'm not allowed to touch any of their stuff without permission. Their makeup makes me look way older than I am, and I try to remember their hip-swaying walk as I approach Jeffery's Lounge. I get past the burly security guards, no problem. It takes a second for my eyes to adjust to the dark. Old, sad jazz songs play on a raspy jukebox. The scent of old-lady perfume is overwhelming. A guy stumbles toward me with a sleepy smile on his face, his feet making a jagged line below him, and I have to dodge his hand when he tries to touch my hair. It feels more like a funeral than a party. I walk past a woman sitting in a man's lap, her hand sliding down somewhere deep under his shirt.

"You see an older woman?" I ask the bartender. "Bad leg?"

"Lots of older ladies with bad legs in here." He laughs. "What's she go by?"

I don't want to say. Embarrassed, I smile.

He sets down a napkin in front of me and then quickly takes it away. "You don't look that old."

I look around one last, frantic time, and then I run out. I check Sula's and Petit Peu's. I check Shoeless Mo's Bar and Grill. I'm going home after Eureka's, I tell myself. Granny'd be happy with this kind of sleuthing.

I'm a block away from Eureka's, and I can already hear the sloppy, high-pitched voices. Inside, everyone is sweating and no one is moving. The floor is sticky, and there's a salty-sweet stench that forces me to breathe through my mouth. I have to cover my eyes from the rainbow strobe lights blinking overhead. Granny loves places like this. My sisters hang out at clubs like this four nights a week. Now, finally, I get it: There's a freedom in the darkness, something about all of the sequins and jewels that makes it feel like a dream, like you're inside one big, pulsing secret.

If Granny's here, I won't be able to find her. There are just too many people, too many shoulders to see past. I watch people get swallowed by a dark pulsing center in front of me. Finally, I get some space. I jump up once, hoping I can see Granny. Straight up, like there's something scary beneath me, like I'm grabbing a rebound.

CHAPTER 5
THE (NOT) FAIR

Today I'm meeting the boys at the fair. Since Granny is still gone, I put up the CLOSED sign on the store's front door and hide upstairs as Ms. Evans tries the handle over and over. When she leaves, I walk to the bus stop at the end of the street, jumping over two, three cracks in the sidewalk at a time. I don't remember it ever being this sunny. I don't remember the breeze ever smelling so clean.

I love the fair. Every summer it rolls into town and plops down behind an abandoned butchery like your noisiest, drunkest uncle. Every last part of it—the Ferris wheel, the sugared funnel cake, the adult-size teddy bears—is way, way, way over the top. You pay your ten bucks at the gate, and after five minutes you've pushed your sister into an ostrich at the petting zoo and everything is worth it. The first time I ever shot a basketball was at the Alameda County Fair. I was four or five, and Granny had to hold me up under the armpits to get the shot off.

Justin, Frank, and Adrian are horsing around near the gate, trying to hit one another with their plastic entry bands.

"Where's Mike?" I ask.

They say he's meeting us in one of the fields in the back, where there won't be any kids trying to get an autograph.

We wander through the maze of kid stuff: the face painting, the scary clowns blowing up balloon animals, the petting zoo. Kids half our size zoom around our legs. When the crowd gets messy and we're about to lose each other, I grab Justin's hand, feeling his limp, sweaty fingers curve into mine. I let go when things open up at the food court. Lines run forty, fifty deep at the ice-cream stand. I can almost taste the cotton candy being spun in a big steel drum in front of us.

Adrian points to a packed area just ahead, where people are lining up for the World's Strongest Man game.

Justin and Frank nod.

"That baseball thing looks fun," I say.

"Baseball?" Justin says. He looks at me like I'm crazy. "You mean basketball?"

I say no, but they chant—"Bas-ket-ball! Bas-ket-ball!"—until people start looking and I have to say yes. I follow a few steps behind them, hoping they'll get distracted by something else, maybe lose me in the crowd. The guy running the basketball game recognizes me instantly.

"No, no, no," he says. He waves a tattooed finger.

"We didn't do nothing!" Frank says.

The guy points at me.

"I'm not allowed to play," I mumble.

"She cheats," the guy says. "And I'm sure you guys do, too. You can't play, either."

He puts his hand over the slot where you put in coins to play. Giant, friendly-looking stuffed animals hang just above his head. Last summer I came here four, five times a night. People would walk over from the food court to watch me shoot, would whistle and hoot and scream insults at the carnies during my hot streaks. I won so many fruit baskets and gift cards they made me pay four times the usual amount to play.

"Damn." Justin whistles after I've told him. "That's the coolest shit I ever heard."

Everyone nods, but I don't feel any better. We're sitting at a picnic table in the back of the fair where the lights start to peter out, right next to the stables where they keep the doomed hogs. The mud smells rusty, and it feels alive, the way it sucks and slops at our shoes. If you squint, you can see the sagging trailers the carnies sleep in just outside the gates. A DJ shouts over the intercom that someone is missing their kid. From the look of the cigarette butts, this is where the carnies chill on their breaks. Every so often a couple of kids sneak off into the true dark behind the porta potties. We're watching the porta potties knock against each other when Mike materializes out of the darkness.

"Gentlemen and lady," Mike says. As always, his voice sounds syrupy, like he's just woken up from a nap.

We give him a round of dap.

"What's going on this evening?" he asks.

Laughter rises in the distance, a noise just as bright as all of the lights. Frank explains the situation: no games because of me. And Justin throws up on rides, so no rides.

"How about there?" Justin points, embarrassed. "That tent."

Right on the edge of the darkness, between our table and civilization, is a sad little tent that looks like it's been left in the rain too long. Every few seconds the walls of the tent turn red from a light inside. We walk over in silence. I lift the front flap and inhale a lungful of smoke.

"Come in, come in!" a gravelly voice calls out to me. And before I can say anything, a spindly arm is pulling me down onto a pillow.

The tent was made for two, three if you're pushing it; we sit in a circle with our knees grinding against one another like gears. Once the flap closes, all our faces are tinted by the bloodred light. The boys look at each other nervously, but I'm secretly smiling to myself, knowing that Granny had a much more believable palm-reading operation during her store's heyday.

"In this day and age, the services of the otherworld aren't free," the lady says. She lights a couple sticks of incense and throws them into the center of the circle. "So who's paying?"

Justin asks how much it is.

"Ah! I knew *you'd* ask," she says,

winking. "Fifteen for one read, thirty for the group."

With how close we are, we don't have to talk if we don't want to. It's in the eyes. Frank wants to go for it, have a little fun. Mike doesn't trust the "energy." Adrian is a no. Why not, I figure. It'll be fun. I think of Granny trying to predict the weather and getting it wrong, wearing a big raincoat during a heat wave. When Justin sees that I'm down, he nods his head and agrees. We pool our money and hand it over.

"Just a little something for the oracle to speak," the lady says. She pulls out her cards and begins flipping them. Her hands are smooth and slippery, like a shoplifter's. She closes her eyes, bobs her head knowingly. "Him." She points at Justin. "That's your boyfriend." She points at me.

"No," I say quickly. My face is suddenly hot. I can't even turn to look at Justin.

"Not yet," she says. More quiet. She asks to see our palms, so we show them to her. More quiet.

Justin asks if she sees anything about him.

"Fire," she says. "I see fire."

Justin, wide-eyed, looks at Frank.

"Okay," I say. "This is stupid. Thanks. But you're not even doing it right."

"I can see," the lady says, her voice quivering, "that we have a doubter in our midst?"

"No. I just know a friggin' scam when

I see one," I say, pulling my hand out of the circle. "Just tell us that our love lives are a work in progress and that we should be optimistic and that our dead ancestors are rooting us on from the grave. Let's keep things moving."

"There's a lot of sadness in you, my love, I can see that."

"Trust me, I'm not the sad one in this situation."

"Okay," she says. "So I bet you wouldn't like it if I told you that the things you have planned—the great things you have planned—are going to hit a few roadblocks."

"Breaking news," I say, angrily. "Life presents a bunch of friggin' challenges."

"And that it's important to be

friendly to messengers of the universe before you find yourself shut out of the doors that open to good fortune."

"Anything else?"

"The bathroom is not your friend." She straightens her cards and adjusts her satin tunic, smirking. "That little bit of advice is on the house."

Outside, Justin looks at his hands for any signs of change. "Probably just stupid, right?"

Everyone nods.

Adrian and Mike peel off on the walk home. The way downtown clears out after midnight, and with the lights changing for cars that aren't there, it all feels apocalyptic. Somewhere far off something is burning; gray ash floats down all around us. Frank doesn't notice that I see him secretly crossing himself a bunch, mouthing a million Our Fathers.

"That was stupid," I say.

"Very," Justin agrees.

"Yup," Frank says.

And then he trips over a crack in the sidewalk and scrapes his knee and starts crossing himself before he gets up. He says his sister told him a story once about an aunt who picked on a psychic cousin and that cousin turned her into a goldfish. Then she flushed her down the toilet. I grab him by the shoulders and ask if he actually believes that. He doesn't look at me.

"I don't know," he says.

"What the hell are you guys afraid of?"

"Nothing," they say together.

From where we are now, the fair is just a point of light.

"There's nothing to be afraid of," I say. "Nothing."

CHAPTER 6

EATEN ALIVE

The microwave says it's 2:14. I can't sleep. I curl up under a blanket on Granny's La-Z-Boy and watch a rerun of *Rocky II*. I watch *The Karate Kid*. Daniel-san just did the "crane kick" and it's still not light out. I do a couple of weak-armed push-ups and stop when I realize I'm wearing out my shooting arm. I spend an hour comparing the strengths and weaknesses of all the designs on my shorts, socks, and shoes.

The address for the tryouts leads me to a dingy-looking gym near the Berkeley marina. It throws a ragged shadow on the old, barnacled boats knocking against the docks. The water gives off a swampy stench. On the way over, my stomach was all knotted, jumping into the back of my throat every time the bus stopped. Now, watching two seagulls fight over a pizza crust, I feel light, confident. *It's just basketball*, I tell myself. Basketball's the same everywhere. You put the ball in the hoop.

When I'm inside, I get in the back of a line of tall, broad-shouldered boys. They are boys straight out of fitness ads: stiff posture, long torsos, overly shiny skin. Their parents stand behind them, brushing lint off their glossy jerseys. They smell like nothing, like their clothes were bought special, vacuum-sealed, just for this. The kid in front of me is listening to his dad tell him how to impress a coach, which you can do apparently by being the first in line for every drill. Inside the gym, there's a girl throwing a ball to herself off the backboard and shooting reverse layups. I don't see the bald-headed guy who invited me, and I start to wonder if this was all a big misunderstanding. As I inch my way to the front of the line, I can feel the courage leaving me like air from a punctured ball.

"Name?" a guy holding a clipboard asks.

"Janae Jenkins," I whisper.

He takes a second to look at me and scans the list, pausing on every name with his finger. Someone behind me grumbles impatiently. Finally, the guy hands me a small gym bag. "Your number's in there.

We start in five minutes."

"Is there a bathroom?"

He jerks his thumb behind him.

There's a web of yellow tape over the girls' bathroom. I push the door, but it doesn't budge. A kid comes out of the boys' bathroom next door, a paper towel balled in his hands. He shoots it into a garbage can next to me.

"Where's the girls' bathroom?" I ask.

He smiles and points down a dimly lit hallway. "I think there's another one down there," he says.

I turn down dark hallway after dark hallway until it hits me that I'm lost. Basketballs echo in the distance, and bare yellow lightbulbs buzz like insects overhead. I lean against a wall and close my eyes. This isn't actually happening. For a second I think about the stupid psychic's prediction—I force myself to ha-ha at the coincidence. Like spirits from the netherworld would care about when you go to the bathroom. *Maybe it's a dream*, I think. Maybe it's one of those disastrous show-up-to-prom-in-your-underwear dreams. I slap myself to make sure, and the sting gives me an angry, sinking feeling in my stomach. I feel too stupid to call out for help, to be the girl needing rescuing on a simple trip to the bathroom. No. I keep my eyes closed and keep my fingertips on the wall. I hear the sound of the bouncing balls echo down the hall as I inch forward . . . until it grows closer, louder, until I can feel the thudding in my fingertips.

I push open double doors that open onto a court as big and solemn as a cathedral. A single shaft of light from the rafters shines onto center court, where a man with a nametag that reads *Coach Tucker* is standing in front of all the tryouts. His voice is megaphone big, bouncing around the gym and echoing by the time it gets to me. It seems like miles and miles of glossy hardwood stretch out between us. I walk across on my toes and take a seat in the back of the group, behind a square-headed kid who I hope makes me invisible.

"This is what's going to happen over the next week," Coach Tucker says. An assistant—the bald-headed guy who invited me—walks up to him with a T-bone steak in a bloody plastic tray. Coach Tucker is surprisingly small, standing there in front of all the adult-boys; his fists clenched at his sides make him look like a kid throwing a tantrum. Then he pulls a steak knife out of his track jacket. Some of the guys in the audience laugh eagerly. "We cut the fat," he says. He slices off a chunk of slick fat and throws it into the rafters, where it sticks to a beam. The coaches standing behind him nod knowingly. "That's going to be some of you. And this piece is going to be another one of you. And so is this piece. We cut the fat until there is no more of it. Our teams are lean. They are mean. We do not play favorites. We do not engage in charity. You will learn, you will earn."

Then it's wind sprints. At first everyone

sprints confidently, our strides long and quick, drumming like heavy rain. We run up and down, up and down, all thirty of us. We run until the ground feels like liquid under us, until some kids stumble to garbage cans to throw up. Bile pools on the back of my tongue. Coach Tucker throws pieces of fat at those of us bringing up the rear. He tells us to quit, to find a sport that rewards standing in one spot, like archery. Parents yell encouragement from the stands, reminding us that quitting is for pussies. *When's the last time they ran like this?* I wonder. Every time I get close to quitting I think about the store, about how the shipments of fat-based facial crèmes always smell like something died. I'm no quitter. The girl who was shooting layups earlier stays at half-court during the water break.

"Hey," I say. I want to tell her about the bathroom situation, but she scoots away and puts her headphones in.

Maybe she's shy. She'll get desperate and ask me at some point, when her bladder's so full she can't keep her legs still.

"I think I left my water bottle outside!" I shout. Then I sprint out behind the gym and take a leak in a lovely little spot behind a Dumpster.

The next morning something weird happens. I slip as I get out of the shower and twist my ankle. I'm more angry than hurt. I've stepped out of that shower every summer for the past ten years; I'm no klutz. I hate that I even think about the psychic, but

I do. While I try to tape up my ankle with duct tape, I can't help picturing her leathery face frowning smugly. By the time I get to practice, my ankle's so swollen I have to loosen my shoelaces. It throbs as I run, and now I'm bringing up the rear, dodging the pieces of fat Coach Tucker throws at my feet.

"Just quit!" he says. "Nothing bad about quitting!"

When a kid quits, Coach Tucker sends him off with one of his steaks as a reminder of what he could have had. Our numbers have dwindled from thirty to twenty. Kids collapse on the side of the court, their cramping legs splayed out stiffly in front of them. Kids have walked off the court crying, their broad shoulders pumping like pistons. We never even touch a basketball. While we run, Coach Tucker tells long stories about the Caribbean vacations he's taken with his famous coach friends and their wives.

"You're still here!" he yells at me. "If you're going to be here, don't bring up the rear!"

"My ankle," I wheeze.

He laughs. "You should be more like eighteen here!" That's the other girl's number. "Look at her go! Why aren't you more like her?"

She's on the other side of the court. She always lines up as far away from me as she can; I know more about the back of her head than I do the front. During a break, I corner eighteen near the water fountains.

"What's up with you?" I whisper angrily.

She looks over my shoulder for a way to escape.

"I'm right here," I say.

"I'm trying to make the team," she says.

"So am I. So let's stick together, right?"

"Sorry," she says, sliding away against the wall, "I'm not here to make friends."

We see the light on day four. Fifteen of us have survived; only ten of us will make it. Now, for the first time, we do drills: drills on defensive stance, drills on defensive rotations, drills on offensive spacing. The coaches move us around the floor like chess pieces. Move here, close out on the shooter, except if the offensive guy goes to the key, then you have to step up and cut off the lane, but if they swing it . . .

I'm trying to remember all the drills when Coach Tucker asks for a volunteer, someone to show him all the rotations.

I am standing at one end of the line, slightly bending my knees, trying to be small.

"Anyone?"

If we make eye contact, I know he'll pick me. I look up at the rafters.

"Janae? How about you give it a shot."

I have to force my feet to move onto the court. Five boys whip the ball around, but I stand in the middle of them, unmoving.

"Ah," Coach Tucker says, "the old traffic-cone defense!"

The laughter is eager and howling.

"Everyone give Janae a round of applause." He waves me off to the sideline.

"Who brought her here? Was it you?" He points to the bald-headed coach. "You see what happens when you try to be nice?"

I pretend to wipe the sweat out of my eyes so he can't see me cry. After practice I walk to the bus stop, stomping through the tall crabgrass, watching car after car of the other players pass me. *What's wrong with you, Janae?* All I can think about is Ms. Higgin's lesson on *Flowers for Algernon* last year. She made us read upside down and backward to replicate what it would be like to lose a skill we'd had our whole lives.

Behind me, I can hear someone cutting through the grass. The bald-headed coach is slapping at it as he jogs.

"Hey there," he says, gasping. "Going home?"

"Yup," I say.

"How's it going?" He's got his hands on his knees. "How you feeling?"

"Great."

"Really? I thought you'd want to talk about what happened in there. It looked rough."

"That? Nah, that was nothing. Never felt better."

"Are you sure? Because if you need some help understanding things, or how they work, that's what we're here for."

In his voice I hear Ms. Higgin's nagging. She's always badgering failing students to get tutoring after school.

"No, I'm good! See you tomorrow!"

My bus comes late today, and when I

get here a piece of fat whizzes by my head. Today, finally, is a shooting day. Carts of basketballs are lined up around the three-point line. I have to stop myself from doing a cartwheel, from kissing one of the balls. The other kids take turns shooting in front of the coaches, sprinting to the three-point line, then the free-throw line, then the corner, until they've shot an entire rack. Twenty balls.

Eighteen, the other girl, is deadly, and even though she wants nothing to do with me, I feel pride watching her hit shot after shot. Even Coach Tucker lets out an approving whistle. Now it's my turn.

"Whoa, whoa, whoa," Coach Tucker says.

I ask him what the problem is.

He grabs the ball out of my hands. "You

don't just get to waltz in whenever you feel like it and chuck up jumpers."

Now I'm mad. I try to snatch the ball back. "My bus was late."

"If I had a nickel for every time some loser's bus was late, I'd be living in Cabo drinking mojitos! But maybe there's a secret group of bus drivers conspiring to make every loser's bus late. Maybe every time some loser gets to the bus stop, a light goes off and the bus driver has to slow down a little. Is that what you're saying?"

"I don't see you out here hitting any jumpers! You ain't doing no wind sprints! You ain't done shit except stand here with your stupid steak and shout!"

Coach Tucker grins. He takes the other

tryouts to another court. I stay back on purpose, shooting the balls on every rack until I'm done. I make eighteen out of twenty.

Today is cut day. One by one we'll be called in to Coach Tucker's office somewhere in the gutter of the gym. We wait in the bleachers, biting our lips, staring at our shoes, until we're called. So far one kid has walked out with his head in his hands, and three kids have walked out with yearbook smiles. Then the girl goes in. Fifteen minutes later she comes out, smiling for the first time since the tryouts started.

"You're up," she sings to me.

I know I should be happy for her, a girl like me, a girl who makes beating boys look easy, but all I want to do is punch her.

Coach Tucker's office smells like Ben-Gay. There are pictures on the walls of him shaking hands with famous coaches: Pat Riley, Bob Knight, Rick Pitino. Framed next to the pictures are odd inspirational quotes: "There Is No Try in Championship"; "I Would've Cut Judas on the First Day"; "Coaching Is 90% Strategy and 100% Motivation."

He kicks his feet up onto his desk. "Pretty great, eh?"

I look around and nod.

"Okay," he says, folding his hands behind his head. "A team is in many ways like a hand, like an organism, if you will. An organism that needs all its parts to function competently—the riboflavins and nucleotides. And a great organism must also be lean and free of fat. Are you following me here?"

"I didn't make the team," I say.

"No," he says. He pulls out a wrinkled blue shirt. "But we'd like to give you this as a token of our appreciation for your hard work and dedication."

"Tell me why, at least. Why did you cut me?"

He leans back, looking confused. "Janae: You just weren't good enough."

CHAPTER 7
HOOP NIGHTMARES

I know I'm dreaming, but it feels too real. I'm in the store painting lamps a rusty red, trying to pass them off as antiques. When I lean over to paint the bottoms, my drooping boobs tap the floor, making the dust dance. I smell my fingers and they smell like old nickels, and for some reason that makes me happy. So happy that I go outside and ogle the bodybuilders I've hired to stand outside my store and rip foam numbers in half with their bare hands so that everyone knows we're slashing prices. "Worth every penny!" I shout at them, sounding like Granny. Back inside there's somehow a piping-hot pan of beef lasagna sitting on the counter. I eat it with my hands; the meat sauce runs down to my elbows. One of the bodybuilders opens a beer using his nipple, and I drink it down. When I'm done, he bows and breaks the bottle on his head and thanks me over and over. I look down at my half-eaten lasagna, which now has pieces of glass in it. I keep eating.

When I wake up, I stay awake for as long as I can, pinching myself, for once glad to feel the pain.

CHAPTER 9
LIFE AFTER DEATH

I don't know how long I've been lying in bed. I spend whole timeless chunks of the day asleep. My dreams float above me like a black cloud, a kind of velvety curtain a couple of inches from my face. I like feeling nothing. I pull the covers even higher, all the way to my chin. Now the sun is high in the sky, but I have no idea what time it is. All the sounds of the day—the sirens, the seagulls, the car horns—they're all blurring together into a sound that feels like a needle behind my eyes. Then I hear a sharp tinkle against my window. I hear it maybe a dozen more times before I realize I'm not dreaming.

Justin is on the sidewalk, holding a handful of pebbles.

I throw open the window. "You almost broke the glass," I say.

"Sorry," he says, dropping the rest of the rocks.

"What is it?"

"Where you been?"

"Busy."

He kicks some of the pebbles into the street. "We were wondering."

I can feel my headache getting worse, the needle behind my eyes sharpening. "I'm fine."

"Got it."

He's smiling up at me like a newborn, all innocent and well-meaning, and suddenly I'm overwhelmed with anger. The night at the fair comes back to me. The way I remember it, Justin forced us to see the psychic. So what if I don't believe in all of that? What if it did something? What if that's what made me turn my ankle and made my bus late? What if that's what got me cut?

"We're playing in Berkeley again tonight," Justin says. "You want us to meet you here at seven?"

"No," I say. He winces at the sharpness in my voice, and something about that makes me feel better.

"Well, what time then?"

"I'm not coming."

"Oh okay. Okay, I'll just come back tomorrow then."

"Don't. Just stop coming."

Justin looks down at the sidewalk and then up at me. "Did I do something?"

"I don't hoop anymore, and if I did, I wouldn't hoop with your lame asses." I slam the window shut and lie back down. For the rest of the afternoon I listen to the pebbles plunking softly against the window.

I don't know when I fell asleep, but when I wake up, the doorbell is buzzing. I wait for it to stop, to confirm the worst about Justin, that he's a simp, that he gives up easy, that he never really cared in the first place. But the bell keeps buzzing, and with a little more hope than I expected, I throw open the window and look down at the street.

It's the bald guy from Bay Area Ballers, the one who invited me to the camp in the first place.

"Ahoy," he says, waving. "Can I come up for a minute?"

I try to shut the window, but it's jammed, and I'm too weak to move it.

"I'm guessing you don't like me very much right now," he shouts.

"Who gave you my address?"

"You wrote it down at the tryouts, when you signed in."

"Thanks for that, by the way. Exactly what I needed."

"Okay." He holds his palms out to

me. "That was admittedly not a great experience. Didn't turn out the way a lot of us wanted."

I'm watching a squirrel tightrope walk across a power line, hoping it somehow falls onto this guy's big, shiny head.

"Coach Tucker's lost it, Janae," he says. "He's a nutcase, a dictator. He was saying that next year tryouts are going to be even harder. He's been watching *The Hunger Games* and taking notes."

"So? Why should I care? I'm not on the team, remember?"

"Because he fired me. Because I brought you. So I'm done. And I want to start something new, something fresh. I want you to be a part of it."

"I'm retired."

"I highly doubt that."

"Stop trying. Don't come here."

I slam the window shut and lie down and pull the covers over my head. Bald guy is shouting. He's laughing. He's saying I'll change my mind, so just come find him when that happens.

EXTREME MAKEOVER

Life without basketball isn't so bad. With Granny still gone, I take packs of her rolling papers to the library, where I watch videos and practice making crippled origami birds and insects. I catch up on episodes of *Extreme Food Makeover*, and with the leftovers from my breaded nachos I feed the ducks at the lake. I count the scars on my legs, documenting their size, shape, and degree of brownness, trying to remember where I got them. I watch my sisters' Hip-Hop Abs videos, smirking at all the greasy six-packs. My basketball gear sits in a black bag next to the front door, where we keep trash before it goes downstairs.

The sun rises, the sun sets. A day goes by, then a few days, then a week. My sisters show up on a Sunday, in pink, bedazzled sweat suits, carrying matching pink gym bags. They flop down next to me on the air mattress, nudging me until I'm backed up against the wall. I can't tell what it is they smell like, something sweet and heavy and stale.

"And so I told him, 'I'm not that kind of girl.' And he said, 'Well, what kind of girl are you?' And I said, 'A good girl.' And he said, 'Looks to me like a good girl with a little bad in her.' And I said, 'Are you calling me bad?' And he said, 'If the shoe fits!'"

They scream. Then they turn to me.

"Shouldn't you be out sweating somewhere?"

"Not my thing anymore," I say.

"About time! All those boys and you never had a man!"

I roll over and face the wall. Behind me, I hear them sniffing around until they've put their noses right against my armpits.

"You stink!" they shriek. "You don't take showers anymore!"

I shrug. "I guess it's been a while."

My sisters are Barbies. They are foreign to me, another species, some new dolled-up, busty version of *Homo sapiens*. For as long as I can remember, they have been the pretty ones. Their eyes are straight out of a Disney movie, big and seductive. In high school they were voted "Most Likely to Have a Drink Poured on Them in a Reality Show" four years straight. As kids, they dressed me up like one of their dolls—smearing our mother's lipstick clownishly over my mouth and trying to fit their tights over my gangly legs. I don't understand how we're related.

Suddenly they're up, rifling through their gym bags. Out come the push-up bras and nail files and curling irons.

"Are you thinking what I'm thinking?"

"No," I say. "I'm not getting a—"

"Makeover!"

I pull the covers over my head. "Please.

Leave me alone, y'all. I'm not like you."

But they're already jumping on the bed. "One of us!" they shout. "One of us! One of us!"

A boy whose name I can't remember is telling me about his workout routine. It's an *L* name, I think: Lamar, Lucas, Larry.

"Most people don't know this," he says, "but you have to split your reps into smaller chunks. That way you get more definition."

Lamont, LeSean, Landré, Leroy, Lincoln, Lorenzo, Luke, Leo, Langston, Lateef, Luther.

"Now if you really want to build, then you start getting into proteins, which can be animal-based or plant-based, depending . . ."

He rolls up his sleeve to show me his biceps. Next to me, my sisters are looking at the dessert menu, stopping every now and then to giggle at their dates. It took them forty-five minutes to eat their Caesar salads; they picked at them like finicky rabbits. When I ordered the ribs they looked at me like I'd farted. After we ate, they made me go to the bathroom with them.

"What are we doing?" I asked.

"You think this is easy?" they said, adjusting their bras.

My girdle is killing me. I tell myself that this is better than nothing. And it kind of is: at home I was driving myself crazy, baking gingerbread men with Coach Tucker's face and then chomping their heads off. On the rare nights the twins slept at home, they said I churned my legs in my sleep, like I was running somewhere. I'm grateful to be out of the house, even if that means I have to give up deep breathing.

Now the boy is asking me about my favorite movies. In my fake Louis Vuitton purse I'm carrying a book titled *How to Always Have Something Interesting to Say.* When you don't have anything interesting to say, just ask a question.

"What's *your* favorite movie?" I ask.

"*Scarface*," he says, his eyes bulging.

"Oh. Well, what's good about it?"

"Uh, everything! Al Pacino! And that other guy who's his best friend, the guy with the hot sister."

"Oh, wow. What other movies do you like?"

As he talks I imagine what Justin and Frank and Adrian and Mike are doing. I can't help it. It's Sunday night, which means they should be at Marcus Garvey Park, where you have to fight off the seagulls to get on the court. Mike would probably look for some bread to lead them away, and Frank would demand we take off our shoes so he could throw them. Adrian would smile secretly. Justin would move a step or two closer to me, in case the seagulls made a move. We'd play until they turned out the streetlights and then walk to the corner store and get two-for-one ice-cream sandwiches and sit on the curb and rinse the sticky off our hands in the water fountain.

"Right?" the boy says to me.

"Huh?"

"Don't you think *Scarface* is all about making it even when the whole world is against you?"

I lean back. "I don't know," I say.

He leans forward. "You don't know what?"

"Aren't we too old for favorites? Favorite movies? Favorite colors? That's stupid."

He leans back, throws his napkin onto the table. "You need to get out more."

The twins are relentless. They make me roller-skate. We walk over the crumbling planks of the Embarcadero in high heels. We ask boys for directions on the way to the Berkeley Bowl, even though we've been there a million times and know exactly where we're going.

"Isn't this fun?" they exclaim. They're flat-ironing my hair. Long fingers of vapor emanate from my head.

"Sure," I say. "Ow."

"The price of beauty!"

We're on our way to a basketball game I don't want to go to. We're bunched in the backseat of some guy's mom's car, drinking Jack Daniels out of Solo cups. I can feel the bass of a song I've never heard in my fillings. I can't move my face under all this makeup. My legs jam up against the back of the seat in front of me. There's an ozone-depleting amount of Axe body spray in here. Not even Coach Tucker's camp made me this miserable. One of the twins nudges me in the ribs, reminding me to look like I'm having a good time. I smile.

"*Woo-hoo,*" the twins shout, and we all drink.

By the time we get to the court I'm so drunk that I'm sure I'm there to play. I reach under my skirt and start undoing my girdle straps. I grab the twins by the arms, ask them for my shoes, my lucky shorts. I demand they run a couple warm-up laps with me. I want to see their shooting form, their knee bend. They're laughing, and I want to know what's so funny. I want to know what they're laughing at.

"We're getting your team together right now," they say, dragging me into the stands.

I don't like the players on the court, guys who pass recklessly and shoot ugly three-pointers. They don't talk on defense. They are blurring into each other, their neon shoes clashing greens and reds. My stomach is a washing machine. My sisters sit next to me, scanning the crowd as they complain loudly about the cost of nachos. They are too loud, everything is too loud, all I want is a little quiet, a little *shhh*. But everyone keeps talking, and I hate them. The ball sails into the stands and spills the soda of a girl sitting right in front of us.

"*Boooo!*" I shout, jumping to my feet. "*Boooo!*"

My sisters pull me down by my wrists.

"*Boooo!*"

Then someone behind me boos, and another person, and soon a whole chorus of boos spills out of the stands. Everybody on the court is frozen. A deep voice shouts for a new game. A big guy jumps out of the stands and takes the ball. He says he'll be taking things from here. The players walk off the court slowly, looking back with thin, embarrassed smiles, like it's a joke, like they expect us to call them back any second. The crowd cheers even louder. People all around are giving one another high fives.

Then it's two new teams, and I laugh to myself because one of the kids looks like Justin. I mean, he's got the funny gimp in his step and the same long, alien arms. And what's even funnier is that the kids with him look like Adrian and Mike and Frank.

"Hey, Janae!" the Justin look-alike says.
I look around.

"You look different," he says, and it's the eyes—the way they're asking questions he'd never say out loud—that tell me it's him.

"Hi, Justin," I hear myself say. I can feel my arms moving to cover my frilly top.

He tries to spin the ball on his finger. "Catch up after the game?"

He bounces back to the court and points to let everyone know where I am. They all wave.

They pick up a random guy as their fifth. It's doomed from the jump. Frank likes to bring the ball up and hand it off to Adrian, who dances a little before he drives down the middle of the lane. When that happens, I usually slide down to the corner, and Adrian doesn't even have to look at me when he passes it. But their new guy doesn't move like me, and Adrian misses and throws the ball into the stands. That's all it takes.

"Boooo!" someone shouts.

I turn around. People take deep breaths and cup their hands around their mouths. The booing is bitter and harsh, all of it bleeding together into something big and overwhelming. Someone asks for a water bottle to throw at Justin. Someone else wants to know if that's really Mike from that Disney show. Some people jump out of the stands and edge onto the court so they can get a little closer, really be heard. My sisters tug on my skirt, reminding me to boo. I do it, at first quietly, hoping they won't hear me, and then I do it until I'm straining my throat. I do it until I'm out of breath, and I'm surprised at how good it feels to be out of breath again.

The boys watch us. They watch me. They huddle together, tense and confused. They start to jog off the court, into the night, so close together they seem fused at the shoulders. I boo even louder.

CHAPTER 10
CALL IT A COMEBACK

The last thing I remember is my sisters discussing how to get vomit off a chiffon blouse. The next morning, Granny finds me on the floor of the bathroom, my cheek stuck to the linoleum.

"You're back," I mumble.

"I can't leave you alone for a couple weeks?" She sighs. She steps over me and starts running the bathwater. I listen to her splashing happily.

Later, I hear the muffled sounds of her crime shows through the bathroom door.

Every few hours she brings me saltine crackers and ginger ale. When I have enough strength to get up, I crawl to the living room and lie at her feet.

"You happy now?" she says, throwing a blanket over me.

"I didn't mean to, Granny."

"I hope not!"

Her feet are warm and soft and smell like lavender. I fall asleep, and when I wake up, it's night. There's a tiny jackhammer lodged in the front of my brain.

"Please turn down the TV," I whisper.

"Don't drink things you shouldn't drink!" She mutes the TV. "So what caused such stupidity, dear?"

"I was out with the twins."

"Ha! The two of 'em share one brain! You know that!"

I tell her about the basketball tryouts, about the psychic.

She laughs. "Bad luck! You just got beat!"

"What if it *is* my luck? Can't you do something for that?"

"Baby, you can't control luck any more than you can control the weather."

I lay my head in her lap.

"That's your problem," she says. She puts a cool rag on my forehead. "You're good at everything! You don't even know what to do when something goes wrong."

"I shouldn't have quit basketball."

"It's just a game, Janae."

"No it's not, Granny!" My tears are

falling onto her feet.

"Lord," she says. "Don't cry about it! These ain't real problems. If it's so important to you, go fix it!"

Outside, the world feels sunny and new. The last two days have been a fog. I close my eyes and listen to the ice-cream man drive by, his jingle loud and cheery. My basketball clothes are wrinkled from being in the bag so long. When I get to the court in Berkeley, the bald-headed coach is busy hustling some kid. He's pulled his socks up to his knees.

"I want to talk to you," I say.

"You look terrible!"

"It's urgent."

He drops the ball, and we walk to a

corner of the bleachers.

"I want to play ball again," I say.

He leans in. "And?"

"I want a coach."

"And?"

"You're my only option."

"Okay then!" he says, smiling. "I'm honored, and I promise with all of the coaching power vested in me that I will never let you down or in any way—"

"Okay, okay."

"Now I just need to start putting together some pieces around you."

"Who you got so far?" I ask.

"Well, I've got a couple things in the works that I'm hoping come through in the next few weeks, really just a matter of time—"

"How many players?"

"As of now? Nobody."

"I got a team already."

"Great, bring them here."

"No," I say, "you have to come with me."

The leather seats in Coach Wise's pickup are cracked. Pieces of leather cut into my back and my butt. Coach Wise drives with both hands on the wheel, slowing down to a stop at the yellows and accelerating smoothly on the greens. Since it's Friday night, the boys will be at a quiet little court near the Coliseum, a court we practiced secret plays on in case we ever needed them in a close game. It makes me nervous that he isn't nervous. I stick my head out the window and let the air punch me in the face.

"Why do you want to coach basketball so bad?" I ask.

"You know what I did for thirty years, Janae?" he asks. "I sold insurance."

"Sounds boring."

"You know how fast time flies when you're doing something you hate?" He snaps his fingers. "Like that. And one day you wake up with no hair, and everything you want in life is out of reach."

When we get to the park, the boys are playing two-on-two. I walk right up to the edge of the court, to the white out-of-bounds line.

"Hey, boys," I say.

"Your ball," Frank says, ignoring me. "Take it out."

"You guys wanna play threes?"

For a second, for less than a second, Justin glances at me. Then he passes in the ball, and they're playing again.

Coach Wise asks if this is normal, the guys ignoring me like this.

"No," I say. I walk onto the court and block Mike's shot. The ball rolls to the fence.

"Does anybody see how weird our basketball is acting?" Frank asks, walking to the fence. "It's, like, moving on its own. Like it's possessed or some shit."

Justin and Adrian and Mike look at their shadows. I look at Coach Wise. He jogs to the center of our circle.

"Maybe I can help?" he says, extending his hand. "Coach Wise."

"Who's this guy?" Justin says.

"He wants to coach us," I say.

"Who's 'us'?" Frank says. "And what do we need a coach for?"

"If I may," Coach Wise says. "What I'd like to do is take you guys to the next level."

"The next level of what?"

"Well, maybe you're unhappy with your current situation, which requires that you always go to different sketchy courts not knowing what's going to happen. Maybe you'd like to have a more stable playing environment. Maybe you'd like a little more exposure for all of your hard work."

"So you're saying we might get paid?"

"Well, there are certainly many types of rewards that come with playing inside."

"What do you think?" Frank asks, nodding to Justin.

Justin looks at me. Maybe I've never seen him before until today, I think. He's making me feel small, naked, exposed.

"Let's do it," Justin says, throwing the ball to me.

Frank, of course, rolls his eyes.

CHAPTER 11

EXTRA CHEESE

Coach Wise keeps a book titled *The ABCs of Teamwork* under his arm. He reads with his finger, mouthing the words silently. For a week, we don't go anywhere near a basketball court. Instead we do the human knot in a dewy field at sunrise. We stand in a circle and play "telephone" under a noisy overpass. At Tilden Park, we walk single file, all of us blindfolded except the leader, who leads us around thousand-year-old oak trees and evergreen shrubs. Coach Wise asks us to sit in a circle and share our deepest fears. Nobody says anything.

"The team," Coach Wise shouts. "The team! The team!"

What team? I wonder. Frank won't even look at me. Justin stands between Adrian and Mike so he won't hold my hand in the human knot. At the end of the day, we take the bus together and I sit in the front by myself, listening to old nurses talk about their grossest patients. I've never felt so lonely around friends. I watch them greedily, laugh with them when they pull the stop-cord and the bus driver curses so loud the nurses shake their heads and cluck at him. I know the boys hate me, but I'm so glad to be near them, they could ignore me for the next hundred years and I wouldn't care.

"I can see how close you guys are getting," Coach says after we do a trust fall. "Don't you guys feel closer?"

We all look away. The boys had caught me an inch above the ground, so close I'd braced my hands for impact.

"That will be the key to our success! The team, the team, the team!"

Today we pile into Coach Wise's pickup and head over the Bay Bridge into San Francisco, up and down the hills, through the narrow zigzagging streets, until we can see the beach. I zip up my jacket. It's chilly, not beach weather. The ocean is gray and churning; nobody's in the water. There's a stinging saltiness in the air. Stray dogs sniff at the garbage cans, fighting off the seagulls for the best scraps. Sand swirls in circles, biting our naked shins.

"Can't beat this!" Coach Wise says, stepping on a rotted tree branch.

"What are we doing here?" I ask.

He doesn't answer. We walk onto the beach behind him, our sneakers sinking unsteadily into the sand. Coach Wise takes off his shoes and walks to the waterline.

"The greatest team of all," he says, looking down at his book. "Water and land. Destruction and creation. Yin, yang. Enjoy this!"

Coach Wise walks back to his truck. The boys stand a few feet away from me, their hands in their pockets.

"What a nut," I say, hoping to get a

laugh. The boys don't answer. I want to kick sand onto their shoes, do something silly, but Coach's pickup backfires. We all turn to the parking lot.

"Okay!" he shouts. He's quickly reversing. "This is your final project! Use teamwork to get back to my house! Think of it as running a fast break!"

Then he drives off, his tires kicking up a cloud of sand behind him. We watch him turn onto the Great Highway and speed down a side street. The waves crash behind us, uninterested, unmoved.

"Shit," I say.

Frank picks up a handful of sand and throws it at the water. "I can't believe we let you get us into this shit."

"How was I supposed to know?"

"Sorry, forgot. Nothing's ever your fault."

"Maybe you'd like me more if I never said anything." I turn to Adrian. He turns away, staring at the horizon.

"Maybe," Mike says, "we want to talk some things out?"

"Shut up!" Frank says to Mike. Then he turns to me and hollers, "You got us run out of the park the other night! You left us hanging!"

I look away. "I didn't mean for that to happen."

"Nobody can stand you. You're an asshole. We just like you because you're good."

I turn to Justin. "You're just gonna let him say that?"

Justin shrugs and looks away.

I could punch Frank in his miniature-ass mouth. I could throw him into the ocean and watch him bob like a buoy. But he marches away, toward the parking lot, kicking at the seagulls in his path.

"Come on!" he shouts.

Instead, Adrian sits in the sand.

"Maybe my opinion doesn't matter," he says, "but I don't wanna pick sides."

Justin and Mike look at each other and then sit down next to him.

I stand over Justin. My shoes are dangerously close to his fingers. "And what?" I ask. "You're staying with him?'"

"Yes," he says.

"Whatever," I say. "Have fun freezing."

I head to the park across the street.

Frank disappears down an alley a few blocks away. I don't care what happens to any of them. What I need is to get a lift back to the East Bay—but after an hour of sticking out my thumb, I still don't have one. I spend the last few moments of daylight at a gas station, asking people for rides. They get in their cars and lock their doors. There is no sunset: The sky goes from light gray to black in an instant. Lights begin blinking on in apartments across the street. When I get close I can hear the voices of kids, the sounds of plates and microwaves and TV laughter. Fog blindly gropes its way inland. I take shelter in a bus stop, but the bus is out of service. The streetlight blinks yellow, and then it dies. I blow warm air into my hands. I'm trying to convince myself I've done the right thing, but I can feel my eyes getting watery. That's when I hear teeth chattering. It's too blurry and too dark to see who it is. I'm wiping my eyes, taking a step toward the other side of the street, when I realize it's Frank. He's got a newspaper wrapped around his bare shoulders. We're silent for what feels like an eternity.

"You want my jacket?" I ask.

"No," he says.

The wind knocks the newspaper out of his hands. I can see the goosebumps on his shoulders. I slip one arm out of my jacket and throw the free half over him. He moves closer.

"Let's go," I say.

We walk back to the beach, our shoulders rubbing, getting warm.

The beach is too dark to go looking for the rest of the boys, and the waves are so loud we can't tell where the sand stops and the water starts. *This must be what oblivion looks like*, I think. Total darkness, all the lights turned off, all the candles blown out, nothing but TV static. Frank and I stand on the edge of the parking lot—right where the glow of the streetlight ends, where civilization ends—and squint vaguely in the direction of the ocean. We call out until our voices crack. Our words are smothered in the liquid churning.

"Maybe they left," I say. I look for a wave, some sea foam. Nothing.

"Maybe," Frank says.

But he keeps calling and I quickly join in, hoping he doesn't think I was trying to give up. Slowly, the boys stumble out of the darkness, first Justin, and then Adrian and Mike, their legs pushing heavily through the mounds of sand, their hands shielding their eyes from the light. They look like they were buried: Sand coats their arms and legs, their cheeks. Without thinking, I start rubbing the sand out of Justin's Afro, and I'm surprised when he leans in so that I can dig my fingers in deeper. I feel something cold dripping on my leg—his shorts are soaking wet.

"The tide kind of snuck up on us," he says, his teeth clacking.

And then comes the thick silence that happens when we're alone and Coach Wise isn't there to tell us what a wonderful team we are. I know I'm supposed to say something, but I don't know what. Granny's taught me to never give a refund or an apology, and so the words feel peanut-butter-sticky in the back of my throat. *They're just words*, I tell myself, but the thought feels too much like a lie to take it seriously.

"It's cold," Justin says. He's jogging in place to get warm.

We walk a couple of blocks inland, following the smell of baking cheese to a rundown pizza place. One of the flour-dusted cooks recognizes Mike and lets us in after he autographs twenty pizza boxes. We huddle around the oven. I hold out my hands greedily, as close to the fire as I can get without burning myself.

After a few minutes I start sweating, but I can't tell if it's because of the heat or because the silence is back. I know that sooner or later I'll have to explain myself. A bell rings, and a guy comes running over with an uncooked pizza. We scatter, bumping into buckets of flour and steel drums of marinara sauce. He shoves the pizza into the oven, glaring at us as we reconvene in front of the flames.

"I understand if you guys don't want to be cool with me," I say, because I've given up, because the right words won't ever come out.

"We do," Justin says quickly. He doesn't

take his eyes off the flames. "But you never said anything about what happened."

He looks at me. I look into the fire. "I don't know what to say. Saying sorry doesn't feel like enough."

"What else can you do?"

There's this wise look in Justin's eyes, like he knows what he's talking about, like he's been through something. He looks older than us, and suddenly I want him to hug me, to pat my head.

"I was messed up," I say. "I thought my life was over. I didn't know you guys would be there that night. I didn't know what I was doing."

Somebody out front loudly orders a supreme, extra cheese, *chop-chop*. The words float between us, ringing around in the quiet.

"I used to eat pizza every day." I sigh. Anything is better than silence. "At this place by my house. My sisters would take me, but then they heard pizza gave you pimples, so they stopped going. I still brought slices home in case they changed their minds, but the next day the pizza was in the trash, buried under some junk mail. It wasn't even good pizza, it was gross, but it always tasted better when you had someone to eat with."

I can't swallow the giant knot in my throat. Why am I even talking about this? "Never mind."

Justin moves back from the fire a little, closer to me. "I love pizza. Even the gross kind."

One by one the other guys nod. There's

a part of me that's thawing out, that wants something as obvious and cheesy as a group hug, something to prove this is real, but you have to take what the defense gives you. I'm glad for even this much.

"Beautiful," one of the fat pizza guys says. He's clapping a wooden pizza paddle against his fleshy hand, creating big clouds of flour. "Really beautiful. Now if you don't mind—get the hell out."

CHAPTER 12
FRESH START

Coach Wise sees us coming from a block away. He peeks out the window, then slams it closed. It's early morning; we got a ride in a taxi. We stuck our heads out the windows to look back at San Francisco, at the skyscrapers gleaming like mirages. The driver kept looking at us in his rearview mirror, like he expected us to jump out at any moment. "What are you thinking?" he yelled, turning up the heat. "Are all of you wacko?"

"Yeah!" we yelled into the wind.

Now we're on Coach Wise's lawn. The grass is beyond dead. His house is a low-slung bungalow with gutters full of leaves, newspapers for blinds. A lawn chair rests on its side, next to an old, shriveled hose.

"Coach!" we yell. "Coach!"

I put my ear to the door. I hear rustling, a chair scraping across the floor, the pages of a book flipping rapidly.

"Coach," I say. "What the hell was that?"

"Back already?" he asks.

"You left us!"

He opens the door. A dollop of shaving cream rests on his Adam's apple. He's in a brown suit and matching fedora. His shoes are buffed to a mirrored sheen. He looks full of pride until he sees us glowering at him, and then he laughs in a kind of frightened way.

"I have seen many things," he stutters. "But one thing you never get tired of seeing is a team coming together. This is cause for celebration."

He starts clapping. We're hungry and tired and thirsty. We walked around an entire city in one night. We peed in dank alleys. We cut our fingers hopping over chain-link fences. We are not in the mood.

"I suggest you explain some things," Frank says, cracking his knuckles.

"I am also very upset with you," Mike says, halfheartedly kicking the lawn chair.

We all nod.

Coach Wise pulls out a trash bag

from behind the front door and leaps off the porch. He approaches us cautiously, holding the bag far out in front of him. I snatch it. He stands back, his mouth in a hopeful half smile. I pull out a bunch of gold-and-blue jerseys. Our names are printed in block letters on the backs. The letters are crooked, and the jerseys are too big when we try them on, sure—but they're ours. They're ours.

At first, we timidly walk around the yard in them, craning our necks to see our names. We trace the stitching. Then we ask people passing by how we look, older people who don't care and tell us so. But by then we're strutting around, taking group pictures with imaginary cameras, doing pretend postgame interviews. If you're not with us, we don't care what you have to say.

"Now," Coach Wise says, "now you look like a team."

On the front of the jerseys is our name: TEAM BLACKTOP.

That way, Coach Wise says, we'll never forget where we came from.

LJ Alonge has played pickup basketball in Oakland, Los Angeles, New York, Kenya, South Africa, and Australia. Basketball's always helped him learn about his community, settle conflicts, and make friends from all walks of life. He's never intimidated by the guy wearing a headband and arm sleeve; those guys usually aren't very good. As a kid, he dreamed of dunking from the free-throw line. Now, his favorite thing to do is make bank shots. Don't forget to call "bank!"